MW00954249

TOMMY JAMES

THE LITTLEST COWBOY IN RECKON

BY MARIA ASHWORTH

Illustrated by Andréa Peixoto Emmerick

Tommy James

Summary: A cowboy's story about wit and determination. Tommy James is small but he knows how to wrangle in a bully like Bo Jones. Tommy James may be the littlest cowboy in Reckon' but he has the heart and determination of a giant. Bullied by Bo Jones, he quickly figures out how to get around this local cowboy. This is the first in the series.

Big Belly Book Co.
Richmond, Texas 77406
www.bigbellybookco.com

Printed and Bound in the United States of America.

ISBN – 978-0692104491

www.bigbellybookco.com
www.mariaashworth.com

Thanks to living in Texas and my cowboy, "Crockett," for inspiring this former New Yorker to write a cowboy story. - MA

For Fernando - AFE

Tommy James was the littlest cowboy in the town of Reckon.

Crawling into small places was easy.

Climbing under tight spaces was a breeze.

Hiding behind tiny things was simple.

He liked being small, until Bo Jones came to town.

Tommy James practiced target shooting with his itty-bitty slingshot.

Bo Jones cackled. "Why, you couldn't hurt a fly with that thing."

Everyone snickered.

Tommy James paid them no mind.

Tommy James sang a wee tune.
The animals were soothed by his voice.

Bo Jones galloped up and heard Tommy singing.

"Why your voice could put a bullfrog to sleep."

His posse hooted and hollered.

Tommy James kicked at the dirt.
"That cowboy is starting to be a burr in my saddle."

Bo Jones watched Tommy James during lasso practice. "Do you need me to hold an itsy-bitsy calf for ya?"

Everyone chuckled.

Tommy James was fit to be tied.
"That wrangler is getting under my skin."

Tommy James headed back to the ranch.
He found his father's ten gallon hat.

He felt prouder.

Tommy James borrowed his brother's boots.

He stood taller.

Tommy James wore his Pawpaw's duster.

He looked bigger.

In town, Tommy James drank his tiny sarsaparilla.

Bo Jones pulled out a chair and sat across from Tommy James. "Looky here, it's teensy Tommy with his tiny drink. Did your mama dress you today?"

Everyone in the saloon snickered.

Tommy James tipped his hat. "I don't like the snide remarks you've been saying about me. I'd appreciate if you'd stop."

Bo Jones chuckled. "Who's going to stop me?"

Tommy James got the courage and stood. He felt bigger, prouder and taller. Bo Jones got up.

Everyone in the saloon froze.

A cowboy burst through the doors.

"Somebody help! The cattle are gettin' away!"

Tommy James headed for the door.

Bo Jones stopped him. "Where do you think you're going?"

"I'm fixin' to help."

"I don't think so. This is only for the *big* boys." Bo Jones pushed Tommy James aside.

Tommy James grew madder than a wet hen. He threw his hat and coat. He kicked off his boots. "These help like rain boots on a duck."

Bo Jones and his posse galloped left. They loped right. They had no luck rounding up the unruly herd.

Bo Jones panted. "No wrangler can get these cows under control."

Tommy James ambled past them with determination.

He tried his lasso.

Too small.

The cowboys snickered at Tommy James.

He used his slingshot.

Too short.

The cowboys laughed at Tommy James.

Tommy James didn't give up.

He knew what he *could* do.

He opened his tiny mouth and sang.

"Down in the valley, the valley so low,

Hang your head over, hear the wind blow."

Tommy sang until one cow swayed left. Another swayed right. Some tip-toed in a haze while others danced in a daze.

They grew sleepy as they followed Tommy James' soothing little voice into the corral.

When he finished singing the herd was fast asleep.

This time no one heckled Tommy James as he headed back to the saloon.

Bo Jones' spurs clanked through the door.

Tommy James thought there might be trouble brewing.
Everyone in the saloon stared at the two cowboys.

Bo Jones' voice softened. "I reckon' I was mistaken. My posse could use a big singing voice like yours in our round-ups. Might you join us?"

Tommy James liked the idea. "Sounds dandy! Barney, two sarsaparillas for me and my new friend."

Tommy James felt bigger, taller, and prouder.

Down In The Valley

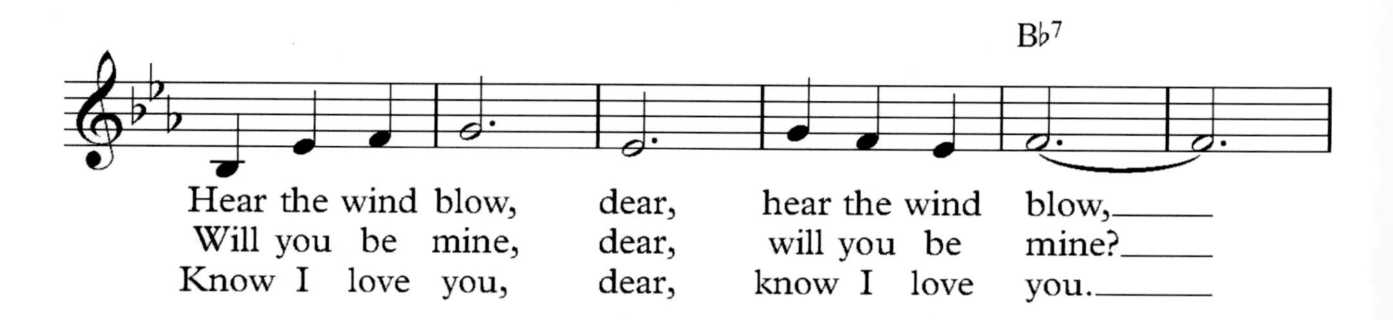

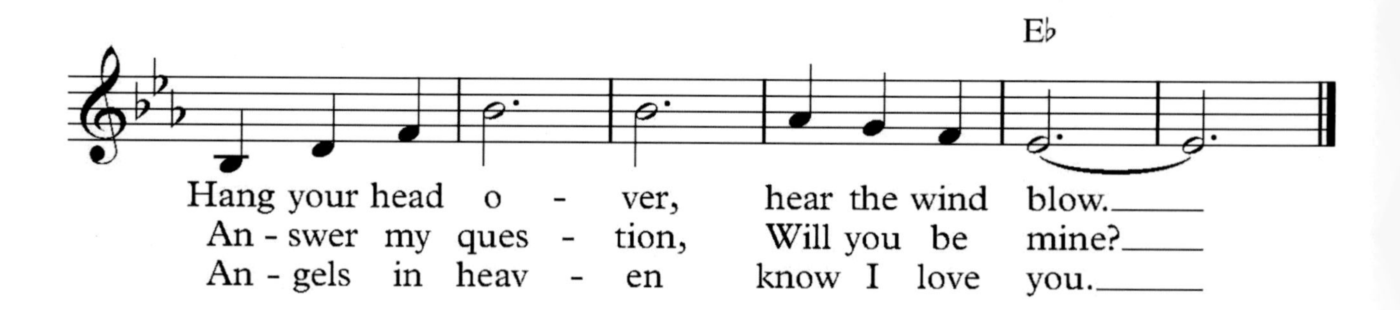

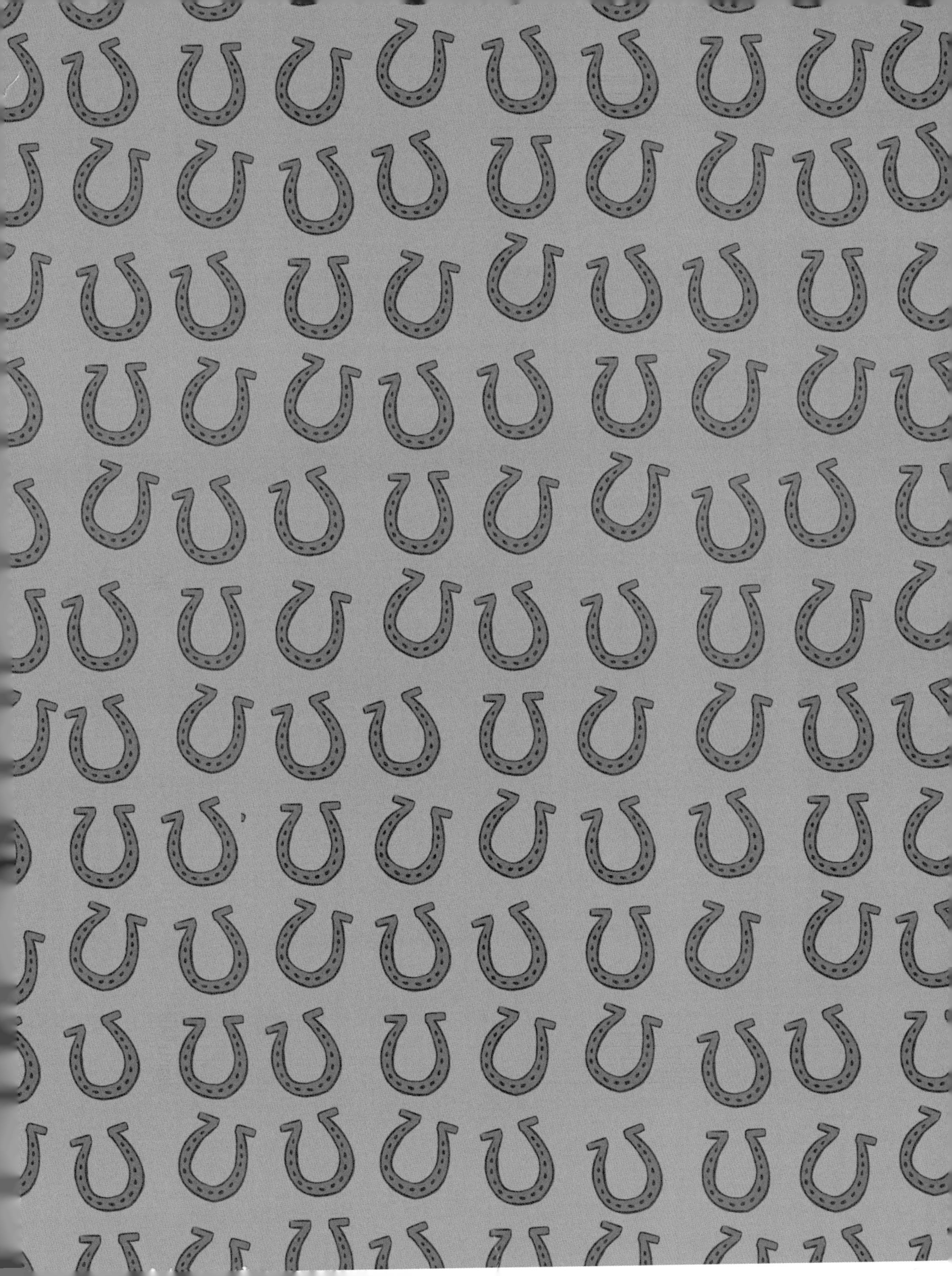